Tales from the Edge of Experience

A Collection of Short Stories & Poems

Helen Mangan

MANGAN PUBLISHING

© 2023 Mangan Publishing
ISBN 979-8-87207-297-3

MANGAN PUBLISHING

To everyone I've met along the way: your experiences and interactions have directly inspired this book. Thank you for shaping my journey.

Table of Contents

A Cup of Coffee

Marcie groaned and rolled over to turn off the alarm. The memory of yesterday came flooding back and the thumping in her head told her that she should not have had that last glass of wine. What a horrendous day yesterday had been.

They had been in the throes of finalising the presentation for today's meeting with one of the biggest tech giants in the business, when it was discovered that one essential component had not been included. This was the responsibility of her boss, but he immediately wheedled his way out of it and managed to lay the blame at her door, and no matter how much Marcie defended herself, the bosses took his word for it. Her co-workers had been incensed but were unable to help, except that at the end of the day they hustled her into the nearest hostelry to drown her sorrows, which she did with great gusto, hence the thumping head.

She rolled onto the other side and closed her eyes, thinking "I won't even go in today" but in her heart she knew that was not an option. She dragged herself out of bed and into the shower. By the time Marcie was dressed, time had moved on and she knew she was going to be late, but quite frankly, she couldn't care. Her joy, which she had always had at going to work had been destroyed yesterday.

Things continued to go badly but she just managed to get her usual train and when she came out of the subway, she saw Starbucks and thought "just what I need, a large black coffee". When she went in, there was a very long queue, but Marcie didn't care. Eventually she got her order and grabbed her cup of coffee and headed out the door. As she came out onto the pavement, she heard the roar of a plane and like so many others looked up to see in horror the plane crash into the North Tower.

"Oh my God" said Marcie "that's our offices". She was absolutely distraught and stood the unable to move. Slowly she came to the realisation that she was safe and as she looked at the cup of coffee in her hands it dawned on her that the long queue and cup of coffee had saved her life.

A Day at the Races

The day dawned bright and clear, and the air of excitement around the village was palpable. It was race day. Each year the local "flapper" race meeting was held on the beach at Rossbeigh. Flapper race meetings were, strictly speaking illegal in so much as they were not governed by any racing body but were traditionally held in several towns and villages in Kerry. The important point about the races in Rossbeigh was that they had to be timed to run when the tide was fully out, and if there was any sort of delay the last race could end up being run through the incoming tide.

I led Biscuit out of his stable and even he seemed to be affected by the air of expectancy. He looked magnificent. His dun coat shining, his tack gleaming and looking like the racehorse he was going to be for the day. We were only entered in the race for local horses, so none of those entered would be heading to Aintree at any time in their lives. That didn't take away from the anticipation of the event. To the participants it was as important as the Grand National.

When we got to the beach there was a huge crowd gathered. The bunting strung all along the beach road fluttering in the breeze. The small funfair was in full swing with the ice cream sellers and the chip vans already busy. Along the edge of the beach the bookies had their boards up waiting for the list of entries to start taking bets. Each horse that arrived was greeted with a cheer, and shouts of "are you worth having a bet on". The excitement grew as the start time got closer, and suddenly it was time to go to the starting line. The course was a straight run along the beach to where there was a pole with a flag on it, and you had to get round this pole and back to the start which had then become the finishing line. There was a lot of jostling as the horses lined up. The starter shouted "ready, steady, go" and we were off. There was sand flying everywhere. It became obvious that if you didn't want to end up being blinded or have a mouth full of sand it was time to put the foot down. Also, we needed to get to the turning flag as close to the front as possible, as that was where most of the "funny business" might happen. I leaned forward and said, "come on Biscuit, let's show them what we've got", and that he did, suddenly we were in front, and it was glorious, the speed was fantastic, and the finish line got closer and closer. We could hear the crowd roaring and the next thing we were through the finish, and I knew we had done it. What a feeling! The only problem was that Biscuit didn't want to stop, and the cliff was looming very close, all I could do was turn him toward the sea and right enough when he got shoulder deep in the sea, he decided it was time to stop. As you can imagine this caused great hilarity with the crowd but Biscuit and I didn't care, we were winners.

A Journey to the Weather Station

On a recent trip to visit my daughter near Montpellier, my son-in-law suggested a trip to the weather station at Mont Aigoual. It was nearly a two-hour drive, and he did warn us that the road we would take was "interesting". We have all seen movies where there are car chases up mountain roads that zig zag up mountains, nearly double back on themselves, well, this was one of those roads. The road literally zip zagged the whole way up the side of the mountain with some sheer drops. It climbs to 1567m, and it was like taking off on a plane with your ears popping as we ascended. It was certainly worth the journey. The panoramic views from the weather station were amazing. We intended to have lunch at the weather station café, but in true French style everything closes down at 2.30pm. Not even coffee was served. C'est la vie!

The one thing I noticed about this beautiful part of France is the number of trees. Any uncultivated land is covered in trees, all the sides of the mountains, and all the towns' longs avenues of beautiful plane trees, and plantations of fir trees, acres, and acres of indigenous trees.

Blast from the Past

It was a big kitchen – and a very busy one. There were large pots boiling on the top of the stoves, the heat from the ovens, preparation areas and people moving purposefully from one area to another. In the midst of all the activity one figure stood still surveying his domain, impressive in his crisp chef's white jacket, topped off by his chef's hat. Ronan took in everything, his eyes flashing from one area to the other ensuring that everything was as it should be. His years of training at the Hotel School in Lausanne had instilled an attention to detail, which helped to enhance his reputation as one of the top chefs in the country.

Tonight's dinner sitting was important, as were all dinners at this busy hotel on the Ring of Kerry, but tonight's guests included ten travel agents from Paris, who Ronan hoped would promote shooting and fishing holidays throughout the winter months. This would ensure that the hotel could remain open for those months.

"Can you bring in the lobsters, Tom," Ronan called to the young pot walloper, the newest addition to the kitchen team. "They're at the back steps". Tom scuttled to the back door, but within seconds he was back ashen faced. "I can't bring them in, sir," he stuttered, "they're alive, one of them is out of the box". Ronan roared with laughter and said, "Of course they're alive," but then he saw the youngster's face and said, "Don't worry. I'll go and get them; you go and help Kitty with the veg". He was still chuckling as he brought in the big box with the lobsters for his signature dish of Lobster Thermidor.

The door of the kitchen swung open and Maeve, Ronan's wife who controlled the rest of the hotel, came into the kitchen. She walked down to Ronan and with the list of the evening's bookings. "Well, you are in for a very busy evening, we're fully booked, oh, bit of bad news though, your new pastry chef has been delayed and will possibly only arrive as dinner starts". Ronan cursed under his breath, this was a real setback, it was the one weak area in the kitchen, and he had been hoping that the new qualified Lausanne graduate, Franz would have arrived from Basle, where he lived, in time to make a difference to to-nights desserts. "We'll just have to manage," Ronan replied and asked if all was well front of house. "No problems," Maeve replied and headed off down the kitchen. Ronan watched as she walked away and pondered on how lucky he was to have Maeve. Since they had married eighteen years ago, they had worked together and built up the hotel to where it was today.

Ronan walked down the kitchen to where Ciara was struggling with the desserts. She looked very flustered and became even more so when he gave her the bad news that Franz would probably not be here in time to help her. He talked to her gently and went through the evening's desserts and little by little simplified what was planned, and when he left her, she was much calmer than before, and everything appeared to be under control.

Meanwhile Maeve dropped into the dining room where the waiters and waitress were busy getting everything prepared: sparkling glasses, gleaming cutlery and crisp white linen tablecloths and napkins. Once again, every detail was checked and re-checked by Elizabeth, the dining room hostess, and she nodded to Maeve to let her know everything was going according to plan. Maeve continued her journey back to Reception, dropping into the comfortable bar with its crackling wood fire. Here everything was also gleaming, and she checked with the barmen, Joe, and Frank that all was well. Both men were all set for a busy evening and said were looking forward to it. Maeve breathed a sigh of relief as she joined Mary, the receptionist at the desk in the lobby of the hotel.

They were going through the bookings when the front door swung open, and a tall fair-haired young man came into the hall with a couple of well-worn suitcases and came up to the desk. "Good evening," Maeve said, "can I help you?" The man gave a charming smile and said, "I hope I can help you. I'm Franz, your new pastry chef, I was very lucky to get the only taxi at the station, so I got here a little quicker than I thought I would". "You're very welcome," said Maeve, I will arrange for Tommy our porter to take you to the staff quarters. Franz quickly said, "If there is somewhere, I can leave my luggage I would like to get to work straight away, I know you have a very important dinner here to-night". Maeve led Franz down the corridor to the kitchen door and announced, "Here's your new pastry chef, Ronan, and he wants to get to work straight away".

Ronan looked up from the final preparations of the thermidor and saw the young man standing beside Maeve. He felt as if he had had an electric shock, and his memory went back to that wonderful summer in Lausanne when he was young and head over heels in

love and he knew that his past was about to come back
to haunt him.

A Major Crime

Bless me, Father for I have sinned. I'm here, Father, to confess my crime. I really don't know why I did it. It was a perfectly normal day, and I had no intention of doing anything out of the ordinary. I went into the shop and was at the magazine rack. I really wanted a particular magazine, but I had no money. It was all so unfair, never having any money, and I felt really angry with the injustice of it. I left the magazine rack and, honestly, Father, I don't know what came over me. Mr. Morris went to answer the phone and his back was towards me, and before I knew it I had slipped a giant gobstopper in one pocket and a bar of chocolate in the other, and I was just about to pick up a copy of the latest Dan Dare magazine and was heading for the door when I was caught by the scruff of the neck and hauled in front of Mr. Morris. I hadn't heard Mrs. Morris come into the shop behind me.

I don't know what came over me, Father and I am really sorry for my crime. And, Father, could you give me a really big penance so that my father will believe that I really told you, as he's waiting outside.

Confession

Once you made your Communion, we were sent to Confession every week. I ask you what sins can a seven-year-old have? Anyway, what happened was that we all knew we told lies. Most of them so harmless they weren't worth thinking about. Being disobedient was another great one, and then laughing in the chapel, which let's face it was not a sin, but we couldn't think of anything else. Then you had to decide how many times! So, the patter went so – "Bless me Father for I have sinned, it's a week since my last confession. I lied 10 / 15 / 18 times, I was disobedient 5 / 8 / 10 times, and I laughed in the Church however many times". And then you would wait for your penance which was usually three Hail Marys. Then we'd come out and go down the back of the Church to say our penances and guess what - the giggling would start again.

A new priest arrived in the parish, and we all piled into the seats for his confessional to give him a go. Mary and I were the only two left to go. We were both sitting to go into the same side of the confessional, when the priest door which was in the middle of the two confessionals burst open and Father Baker appeared and said, "are you two girls going to sit there all day, wouldn't you have the sense to go one on either side". Well, we nearly died because in our books that wasn't playing by the rules. The priests were not supposed to see you and know who you were!! Anyway, I went in and started my rote. He immediately spoke over me and said, "Tell your sins". Now this also wasn't playing to the rules, and once I couldn't do my "Bless me Father" bit I was completely thrown. I set off again and he immediately jumped in saying "Tell your sins". So, I got desperate and just blurted out my rote and took no notice of him saying "tell your sins". From this day forward, he was off our list for going to confession to.

The one good thing about him was that he was an awful lot faster than any of the others. He had been in America before he came to Bray and he started to reorganise things and took overlooking after the altar boys and it was like a military operation, they walked in step, they shook the incense holders in time, they turned to the right or left like a platoon of soldiers. He became known, very disrespectfully, in our house as Hidel Didel Baker and his Thump Thump Boys.

Dingle Bay

The village of Glenbeigh nestles at the foot of the Seefin Mountains, on the Ring of Kerry. It was here that the Riding School I worked in was situated, and from where we ran pony trekking for visitors who came from all over the world. One particular trek went over the Seefin Mountains. We would set off from the village and take the track up the mountains. About three quarters way up the trail there was a wide space where it was possible to stop and look back and take in this view, and what a view. Spread out before you was Dingle Bay with the Dingle Mountains in the background. In the foreground was Rossbeigh Strand which is three and a half miles of beach and sand dunes and stretching from the far side of the bay is Inch Strand which is nearly seven miles long. Between the tips of these two beaches the sea surges into Castlemaine Harbour. It doesn't seem to matter what the weather is like this view is always stunning, whether languishing in bright sunlight or being swept by soft Kerry rain and clouds scudding across the horizon.

When the trek reaches the top of the mountain, and you ride over the crest there is an outstanding view of Caragh Lake in the foreground overshadowed by the Macgillycuddy's Reeks and Carrantuohill dominating the scene. As the ride wends its way along the side of the mountain the view changes all the time as you see more of the mountain range or further up the Lake. A lot of this mountain side is not only covered in gorse, but at certain times of the year there is an abundance of rhododendrons, giving a riot of colour across the mountainside.

When we get to the shores of the Lake, we stopped in the O'Sullivan family's lovely, thatched cottage, where we are welcomed by the lady of the house. There, in the cottage, in front of the big open fire where Mrs O bakes and cooks, we partake of freshly baked soda bread and free-range boiled eggs, with large mugs of tea. Never did a meal taste so good.

Discovery

The panoramic view of Lower Manhattan from her office window was lost on Monique as she sat at her desk perusing the daily papers which were spread out in front of her. She had made the headlines as lead prosecutor on the biggest fraud case in years and she had nailed it. She had been catapulted to the top of her profession, and the world was now her oyster.

But instead of feeling elated Monique just felt tired, bone weary, in fact. She had put in hundreds of gruelling hours on this case, and it had paid off, but at a price.

She thought, "What I need is a break away from all of this, and a chance to recharge the batteries". Various options ran through her mind, and as she moved the papers from her desk an advertisement caught her eye. The heading read - "Ireland Awaits," and then, "come and visit Glen Farm Cottages in Ballyheigue, Co. Kerry, Ireland". This is kismet, thought Monique. For some reason she had always wanted to visit Ireland, but her parents were very much against the idea whenever she had suggested it. Now that they were no longer there it seemed that this was the time. Her heart still felt as if it would break when she thought of that night when the cop had arrived at her door with the horrifying news that her parents had hit a sheet of black ice when coming home from a weekend in the Hamptons. It had taken a long time to get over the shock of their sudden deaths, and she still missed them dreadfully.

Through security and heading for the gate, Monique could not believe she was on her way. Once she had made up her mind everything happened so fast and here, she was on her way to Shannon, a hire car waiting for her to collect at the airport and on to a beautiful cottage booked in Ballyheigue.

Monique found it really strange driving on the left-hand side of the road, but once she got used to it, she was able to relax and enjoy the beautiful countryside she was driving through. "Oh my God, it is so green" she thought, "I had heard that it was beautiful, but the reality is even better".

After two hours driving, she saw a sign which said, "Welcome to the Kingdom of Kerry". She felt a smile spread across her face. Somehow her heart took a little leap and she thought, "I feel as if I'm coming home".

Her GPS warned her that she was approaching Tralee, which she was to bypass, and then on to the road to her destination, the seaside town of Ballyheigue. As she came into the outskirts of the town she thought "I must stop to get provisions for the cottage", and seeing a space in front of a supermarket she pulled in to park. She wandered round the supermarket picking up items some of which were unfamiliar, like Carrigeen Moss and Dubliner cheese, but which looked really interesting. With the shopping paid for, she came out on to the street with her trolley and crossed the pavement to her car. As she opened the trunk a voice said, "Here, Monica, let me help you with those," and two strong hands lifted the bags out of the trolley and plonked them in the trunk. Monique turned round to see a tall man striding off down the pavement away from the car, saying over his shoulder, "like the new car, Monica," and before Monique could say anything, he disappeared into a hardware store further up the street. Monique was speechless, it had happened so quickly she had not had time to react. Why had he called her Monica, and why had he acted as if he knew her? She got back into the car and with the help of the GPS was soon turning into the entrance to the Glen Farm Cottages.

She drove up to the parking area in from of Reception and got out of the car. She looked around approvingly. Neat, pretty cottages stretched down to the sea. She turned and opened the door to the reception area. A woman standing behind the desk turned round as she heard the door. Monique stood stock still, all the breath went out of her lungs. She thought, "I'm looking in a mirror" but then the image moved forward, also looking shocked "My God," Monique whispered, "this isn't real". The two girls stood there transfixed. A door opened behind the reception desk and a small plump motherly woman bustled through and catching sight of the two girls, turned sheet white. "Oh dear God, I knew this would happen one day, I hoped I might never have to deal with this. I thought if it ever happened it would be your parent's job, but now that they are not here it falls to me".

"Could anyone please explain to me what is going on and who you people are" said Monique. "I feel as if I've stepped into an alternative universe".

"Of course, my dear, I'm your Aunty May," the woman said, coming over to Monique and taking her hand. "You must be completely bewildered. Come over here and sit down, you too, Monica, and I'll tell you the whole story".

Dust Thou Art

It was Saturday morning, and time to get up. The visitors would be arriving tomorrow, and everyone was expected to help in the clean-up in preparation for their arrival. Matilda was really fed up as all her friends were heading to the beach to go surfing and then following it with a bar-b-cue, and here she was, stuck doing housework. Anyway, best to get on with it, she headed downstairs to get her "cleaning orders". However, it was not only the inside of the house that had to be cleaned but outside as well, and Matilda's first job was cutting the grass. "I don't see why we can't have a ride on mower like the Barton's". Matilda's Dad looked at her with some amusement, "The Barton's garden is nearly quarter of an acre, if you used a ride on in our garden you'd be out through the hedge before you knew it". Matilda continued to grumble, but eventually finished the lawn, then it was clipping the hedge. These jobs were taking so long that any hope of making the beach was fast fading.

After a quick lunch it was on to the housework. Matilda was getting thoroughly sick of the smell of polish, it seemed to have seeped into her skin, but gradually everything was done, when her father said to her, "Now what about your bedroom, Matilda". Oh, said Matilda, "I did that before I came down this morning". Her father looked at her sceptically and said, "I'd like to take a look, please". Matilda had made her bed but that was about it. Her father knelt down on the floor and looked under the bed, he turned to Matilda and said "you know the saying dust thou art and to dust thou shalt return, well just to let you know that there is someone both coming and going under your bed.

Flash Fiction

Spring had come and the grass was ready to grow again. But when the blade of grass pushed towards the surface, it met resistance. A voice came from the pebble above "Hey stop pushing, this is my spot". "Oi, I need to get to the surface roll over and give me that space". "No chance, I'm not moving, grow sideways". The blade of grass was getting desperate, when another voice said "Oh dear, look there is a pebble here on the grass that wouldn't do the mower much good and with that, in a flash, the resistance was gone.

Hannah

You are the piece of silk
That ripples and flows
Soft and light to the touch.

You are the blue of the
Tropical ocean flowing
Across the golden sands.

You are the cherry blossom
As it falls like snow
In the April breeze.

You are the deep red
Glass of wine
To be savoured and enjoyed.

You are as haunting as Finglas Cave
Soaring and swooping round
The rocks.

You are the bright shaft of light
That brightens our lives.

I Had a Dream

I had a dream that one day I would represent Ireland in the Aga Khan show jumping team at the RDS Horse Show in Ballsbridge. I started at the bottom, cleaning out stables, grooming, plaiting and being a general factotum for the local riding school. Bit by bit I get enough recognition of all the hard work by being given free riding lessons. I saved every penny for my horse fund I could from pocket money, wages, tips working as a waitress in the local hotel and from my office job. I spent every waking moment of my weekends and every summer evening at the riding school.

One weekend Mairead, the owner of the stables, said she was going to collect a horse from a local farmer, and I could go with her. We drove up the mountains to a very remote farmstead and while she was talking to the farmer, I wandered off to look around the farm. That was when I saw him. He was standing under a tree in the corner of the field. I called out and he turned his head and looked at me and it was love at first sight. He trotted across to the fence and stopped in front of me, snorting and throwing his head round, nearly like a child showing off. He was black and his coat shone with good health. "Well, that's not something I've seen before", a voice said. I turned to see the farmer standing there. "He is a bit of a handful. We have great difficulty catching him and yet here he is coming straight up to you".

"He's beautiful", I said and before I could stop myself, I blurted out, "is he for sale?"

"I don't think I could sell him to you young lady, as I said he is a handful. In fact, unmanageable would be a better word. I think he's for the knacker's yard".

"Oh no, please, I will give you whatever you for him. Please, I just know he'll be OK".

"I think we should go in and have a cup of tea and talk".

We joined Mairead back in the house and when she heard what was proposed she was very dubious about it but after much persuasion she agreed that I could keep him at the stables but that If there were problems, he would have to go. We negotiated a price which secretly I was delighted with, as it was only half of what I had in my horse fund.

Mairead agreed to bring him home with the other horse if I could get him into the box and he caused no trouble.

I went out to the field with a head collar, and Ebony, which was what I had decided to call him, was still standing at the fence and he whinnied as he saw me approach. I went into the field, and he dipped his head and let me put the head collar on. I led him to the horse box, whispering to him all the time not to let me down and without a hesitation he walked in beside the other horse. "Well, I'll be damned", I heard the farmer say.

We got home safely, and Ebony unloaded quietly, and I soon had him installed in a stable. Then the hard work started. The farmer was right, he was a handful, he was big and powerful and had obviously not had much training. I've never worked so hard but over the next few years, he grew into the most fantastic show jumper, moving up the ranks and becoming noticed by the "powers that be". We travelled the country to different shows and even joined the Sunshine Tour, a European show jumping tour. Then came the day, that the Irish team selector rang, and it had happened. I was on the Aga Kahn team for that year. I thought I would keel over with excitement. They day dawned and the excitement was palpable as were the nerves. Riding into the main area was an unbelievable sensation. The roar of the crowd, the Irish flags waving and then the starting bell. Ebony rose to the occasion and seemed to love the ambiance and played to the crowd coming in with a perfect clear round. After the first round, Ireland was level with Great Britain and the USA. The tension grew as Great Britain had two fences down. Then the USA also had two fences down and Ireland had one, which meant that Ebony had to go clear if we were to win. I entered the arena to a huge cheer. I patted Ebony and whispered, "it's up to us, boy, let's show them". The bell rang and a hush fell over the arena. You could have heard a pin drop. Halfway through the round I heard Ebony's hoof hit one of the poles and I prayed it wouldn't fall but kept going. Then it was the last fence which we soared over and the cheer that went up told me we were clear. Everything was a blur after that and suddenly we were parading for the prize giving. When we lined up after the national anthem was played, we dismounted, and the President approached with the trophy, and I reached out to receive it and then I woke up.

If I Were

If I were a racehorse
I would win the Epsom Derby

If I was an opera singer
I would sing Nessun Dorma in La Scala

If I was an actress
I would play a leading role in a Broadway show

If I was a mountaineer
I would scale the world's highest mountains

If I were an author
I would win the Nobel prize for literature.

But I am none of these things
I am just me.

If I were somebody else

If I were somebody else
I would be bright and enthusiastic
I would be talented and outgoing
I would live life to the full
I would use my skills to entertain
I would give real pleasure to the public
I would achieve star status
I would be Dame Judi Dench

Imagine

"Imagination is everything. It is the preview of life's coming attractions".

How true this Albert Einstein quote is? Growing up wouldn't have been the same without the imagination of Frank Hampson. "Who?", you might ask. Frank Hampson was the creator of Dan Dare, Pilot of the Future. As children we were enthralled by his adventures. We learnt new words like solar system, asteroids, and aliens. We learnt the names of the planets and we looked at the night sky with different eyes.

Hampson's imagination took us to landings on the moon and on Venus where we met the Treens, the reptilian inhabitants of Northern Venus. The highlight of the week was when we pooled pocket money to buy the Eagle comic and see what new adventure he had got up to.

Little did we think that Hampson was giving us a preview of that day in 1969 when Apollo 11 landed the first two humans on the moon, Neil Armstrong, and Buzz Aldrin.

I remember thinking at the time that it was exactly what Frank Hampson's imagination had foretold all those years before.

In Her Mind's Eye

In her mind's eye she could see the golden sands stretching out in front her, with the Atlantic waves tumbling towards them, the froth swirling round the legs of the horse she was sitting on. He jigged about in anticipation, sensing what was to come. The sea breeze ruffled her hair and the horse's mane. She turned him towards the three mile stretch of sand and gathered up the rein. The muscles in the horse's hind quarters bunched as he rocked back ready for the off. She slackened the reins, and he exploded like a bullet from a gun at a full gallop through the surf. The exhilaration coursed through her and as the horse's stride ate up the miles, she saw the brilliant shaft of light at the end of the peninsula. She could see the figure seated on a magnificent white horse who shimmered in the brilliant light, and she knew who it was. In the distance she heard a voice say, "it won't be long now", but she ignored it and surged forward, her hand outstretched and her heart soared as she saw that dear familiar face.

Those gathered round the hospital bed heard her whisper "I knew you'd come", and they watched as her face that had been so drawn with pain smoothed out into the most serene expression and with a deep sigh, she joined the love of her life.

Klickataw

Susan was really fed up; her day had gone from bad to worse. First of all, the potential presidential candidate she had come to interview had put back the time by two hours and then when she went to file the story, the hotel had a problem with its WIFI and though they said it would be back online any minute it took over an hour. Then having filed the story she came out of find she had a flat tire. When she finally got it change it was nearly 8.30pm and she had a five-hour drive to get to the early morning editorial meeting in Boston, and it was essential that she was there.

She set off on the road, and as she did the heavens opened. Driving conditions were appalling and two and a half hours into the drive she was beginning to feel exhausted and was for a service station to get coffee and have a rest. Suddenly she saw lights off to her left, and then she saw a sign for Klickataw ¼ mile and a slip road off the motorway. To hell with it, she thought, I've got to stop. In fact, I might even stop to rest for a couple of hours and set off again.

Susan drove into the town, and it was as if she had stepped back in time. It looked like an old Western town complete with boardwalks and wooden buildings. She saw people going into what looked like a saloon, which was beside Klickataw General Store which was also open. Then she saw a sign which made her give a sigh of relief, the Klickataw Hotel. She parked in front of the hotel and grabbing her overnight bag she went in. The reception was warm and welcoming and the young girl behind the desk gave her a big smile. "Hello, you're very welcome, how can I help you".

"I was wondering if I could get a room for a couple of hours. I'm driving to Boston, but I think I need to take a break".

"Very good idea" agreed the girl. "I'm Charlotte, I'll show you to your room".

"Can I pay you now, as I'm sure you will have gone to bed when I'm leaving".

"No problem just put $40 on the counter when you leave and have a good night" and with that she was gone.

Susan set her alarm for 3 hours' time and lay down on the bed and within minutes was fast asleep. She woke up feeling very rested and got ready to leave. She left the money on the counter and let herself out. She was very surprised to see the town was still busy but got into her car and set off.

She made it to her meeting on time and her editor said "Well done, I didn't think you would make it. You must have driven through the night".

"No, I actually stopped in a place called Kilckataw. It's quite an extraordinary town".

"Well," said her editor, "it certainly must be extraordinary. Klickataw has been derelict for the last 70 years, since the populate was wiped out by a typhoid epidemic. So, wherever you stayed, it wasn't Klickataw".

Lost and Found

I step onto the scales
Eyes tight shut, not breathing
I open my eyes and look at the fateful numbers
There it is five stone LOST

I dance to my wardrobe
Pull out that little black dress
Figure hugging, shape moulding
This is the new me
Self-confidence FOUND

Man of Mystery

He had an aura of mystery around him, at least that was what the locals thought on the few occasions he came into the local village shop. They knew that he smoked, and that he ate bread and drank milk, but little else about the tall dark-haired good-looking man. He was always extremely well, if casually dressed. They reckoned he was in his early 40's which made his solitary existence even stranger. He had called in to the local pub once or twice, sitting quietly in the corner with his pint and his laptop, his demeanour not encouraging any interaction for the locals, and the same applied on the rare occasions he used the local cafe.

Everyone in the village knew that the old O'Byrne cottage at the end of the Coomasalann Road on the lakeside was empty. It didn't even let in the Summer that often as the lake at Coom was a dark brooding place enclosed by high steep cliffs. Mary Mahon kept the place cleaned and aired for the owner who lived in the States but even she had had a phone call to tell her that there would be a new tenant but there was need for her to go to the cottage for a while. This was accompanied by a substantial amount to compensate for her loss of earnings, and this all added to the local speculation about the mysterious stranger.

Then as suddenly as he arrived, the stranger disappeared. No one was aware of this until Mary got a phone call from the States to resume the previous arrangement at the cottage. When Mary got there, it was if no one had ever been there, not a trace of habitation.

Speculation in the village was rife, and the stories became more and more ridiculous, even abduction by aliens.

Some months later Mary went into the local shop, and Mrs Moriarty, the owner could barely contain her excitement. "The mystery is solved", she shrieked and plonked the magazine from the Irish Times open at the middle page. The headline in the literary section read Clam Bartley short listed for the Man Booker prize, and there was a picture of the mystery man. The article said that his new novel was based in a village in rural Ireland, and some of his characters were inspired by a visit to stay in a friend's house in Country Kerry.

Now the speculation in the village was who was going to turn up in the novel.

Mistaken Identity

Cliona was working as a nanny. It was something she had always wanted to do and had been lucky enough to get a job looking after a 6-year-old boy Luke. His mother was a single mum from a very wealthy family who seemed to spend her time travelling between the family properties in various countries. It was a really nice gig.

Luke was a lovely little boy and surprisingly unspoilt considering. After five months in London, they headed for Los Angeles and the Lewis home in the Hollywood Hills. Sounds idyllic but in LA and particularly the Hollywood Hills area, there is no public transport. So, unless Angie fancied an outing, they were stuck.

Angie decided one morning that she was going to have a party that weekend and there was great excitement all week. The caterers were summoned to sort out the food and the party planners to do all the rest. How the other half lives!

On the day of the party, Angie said to Cliona, "I have a special job for you. I have a friend coming tonight called Aaron and I want you to look after him. He's going through a bit of a rough time, so I want you to make sure he's OK. He'll be here at 8 o'clock so make sure you're in the lobby to greet him". Cliona was not enamoured with this assignment, but Angie was the boss.

Guests started arriving from 7 o'clock and at 8 o'clock Cliona was waiting in the lobby. Just then the doorbell rang and as no one else was there, Cliona answered the door. On the doorstep was a tall, very attractive man. "Aaron?" Cliona said.

"Well, yes" he replied.

"You're very welcome, come in".

"Thank you and you are?"

"Oh, I'm Cliona. I work for Angie".

"Do I detect an Irish accent?"

"Yes, I'm from Ireland. Would you like to come through and I'll get you a drink?"

"I'd like that, and you can tell me about Ireland. I've always wanted to visit but never seemed to have the time".

"Well, you should try. It's a wonderful country with lots to do and see".

They got their drinks and chatted away about Ireland. He really was charming and so attractive. Cliona couldn't help wondering what sort of a trauma someone like him could be going through. Cliona said "well enough about me, what about you? You obviously live in LA. What do you do?". He smiled and said, "I'm an actor".

"Oh" said Cliona, "that's great but I bet it's tough. Would I have seen you in anything recently?"
"Well, I suppose you might have".

Just then Cliona saw Angie waving across to her, obviously summoning her and looking a bit cross. Cliona excused herself and went across. "Honestly Cliona, I asked you to do one thing for me and you've let me down".

"What do you mean? I met Aaron as you said, and I've been looking after him. He's over there".

"Oh, for goodness' sake Cliona, that's not Aaron, that's Warren, Warren Beatty. Surely you recognised him. He is the actor of the moment. He's just won an Oscar. Anyway, come on Aaron's over here. You can take over".

Cliona, red faced, turned, and waved to her previous companion. She knew by the broad grin on his face that at least he was amused by the encounter.

Music

We are all familiar with the Shakespeare quote "If music be the food of love, play on". But another powerful quote from German philosopher Friedrich Nietzsche "Without music, life would be a mistake", is possibly not so well known but says it all.

Music is a huge part of our lives, consciously or unconsciously. It starts when we are babies when mothers and sometimes fathers sing lullabies to help with sleep. Then as toddlers there are children's songs like "the wheels on the bus go round and round" and many others. Then on to nursery school and junior school where there is group singing of children's songs. This progresses to school, choirs and then one of the biggest influences on the teenage years, the pop music scene.

At this point, or possibly earlier people start deciding what music they like and there are so many genres – classical, pop, folk, choral musicals to name but a few.

It always fascinates me how music can change the mood and emotion. Watching the Last Night at the Proms, you can feel the emotion when they sing Land of Hope and

Glory, I don't think it's the words as much as the magnificent music. Or at Christmas Mass when the soprano sings "Oh Holy Night" and hits that amazing high note.

One example of this was when I attended a funeral of a dear friend called Michael. Mick to all of us. It was a beautiful service with some very moving eulogies about his life and his love of music, particularly Percy French. The mood was sombre and tinged with sadness as we stood for the coffin to be carried down the aisle. Suddenly the organ burst into the strains of Percy French's "Are ye right there, Michael, are ye right", and people were turning to one another with smiles on their faces, and the whole mood was lifted.

And to finish, one of my favourite quotes, this time from Hans Christian Anderson, "Where words fail, music speaks".

My Favourite Photo

I don't really have a favourite photo. I do have photos that recall the story attached to them, so they are my favourites when I see them again. One that comes to mind was taken while travelling by train from the Mongolian border down through China. The train was a magnificent steam train and the cabins looked like they were from a bygone era. The bunks were pulled down at night and folded back during the day to make very comfortable seats. There was a table between them with a lace tablecloth and a little lamp with a very pretty lampshade.

I don't remember an awful lot of the geography of China from school apart from the capital, Peking as it was then but now known as Beijing and the mighty Pearl River. The name Pearl River always conjured up to me a misty, romantic picture which went with its name. On the second day of the train journey, our guide, Miss Lee, a beautiful, young, and quite shy girl came along the corridor telling us that we were coming to the Pearl River. We all piled out into the corridor from our cabins complete with cameras. As we came towards the river, a little Chinese man who looked about 100 years of age was sitting on the jump seat at the end of the corridor shouted something to Miss Lee. Her face went a little pink and she said "sorry, not Pearl River". We all retired back into our cabins. About half an hour later again Miss Lee came along saying "Now Pearl River". Out we pile again and just as we got ready to click, the voice from the end of the corridor shouted again. This time Miss Lee went bright red and said "Sorry, not Pearl River". Back we go again and when she came along about an hour later, we piled out but when said "now we come to Pear River". We all looked down the corridor to the little Chinese man and with a big smile he nodded his head.

That is why when I look at the photo it makes me smile.

My First Job

After a very solemn interview with the Managing Director, he informed me that I had the job. This was in the day when you had one interview for a job, no such thing of being called back for a second and sometimes third interview. A week later I started as a junior clerk in the Yorkshire Insurance Company in Dame Street. The company had its headquarters in a lovely old building in Dame Street, very near the Bank of Ireland. The entrance had beautiful carved wooden doors which were about 18 foot tall, and these doors were always open during business hours. When you entered the beautiful hall on your right was the Motor Department and on the left the Fire Department, and it was to this department I had been assigned.

When you went into the Fire Department there was a long mahogany counter, and at one end there was a brass grill which was in front of the Chief Cashiers desk. This desk was quite extraordinary as it looked like something out of Dickens. It was a tall sloping desk and the Cashier, a fierce lady called Miss Dormer had to literally climb up onto a high stool to work at it.

All the clerks had a separate desk, and these were heavy wood with leather tops. There were just three phones in the Department, one on the wall for general department calls and one on the Department Heads desk and one on the Cashier's desk. In the corner of the office was a square telephone box where staff were allowed to take and make personal calls, but as everyone could see you go in and out, you didn't tend to make or receive too many calls.

As a junior it was your job, along with taking shorthand and doing typing to attend to the public, when they came into the department. These enquiries could be very varied and sometimes hilarious. For instance, we had a well-known Dublin doctor came in to claim under his household policy for a broken arm, so I asked him to give me details of the accident. He said, "I was sawing a branch off a tree".

"Oh", I said "and the branch fell on your arm?"

"No, no, my dear girl, I was sitting on the branch when I sawed through it".

It showed how well-trained Yorkshire Insurance Company staff were that not a flicker of a smile crossed my face. I bent my head and studiously filled in the details praying that the bubble of laughter in my throat would stay there until he had left.

One day I saw a man in a rain mac and a flat cap at the counter, and I fixed a smile on my face and asked if I could help him. He shouted at me "Is the window cleaner here?".

"Sssorry", I stuttered.

"Is the window cleaner here?" Looking over his shoulder I could see the lads in the Motor Department across the hall killing themselves laughing. "Is the window cleaner here?" he shouted again; this time accompanied with a bang of his fist on the counter.

"No, I'm afraid he isn't" I said, but I was actually talking to myself as he had turned on his heel and left. When I turned around everyone was giggling. "What's so funny" I asked. They explained that he was one of the local Dublin characters, along with Bang Bang, who were well known in Dublin. Sadly, mentally disturbed but looked on kindly by everyone as local colour.

At that time, we used to work three Saturday mornings out of four in the month, and if you were late more than three times in the month, unless you had a very good reason, you lost your Saturday morning off.

When I handed in my notice after a year, my boss said he would really miss me, particularly my excuses for being late, as he said it was amazing how it would be snowing in Bray when it was perfect in Dublin and how the bin lorries always seemed to jam up the traffic on the road I was travelling. He was obviously a very kind man because most the time he accepted the excuses.

For this 9.00 – 5.30 job, I got the princely sum of £4 a week, and mind you at that time it was considered a good wage. I really enjoyed my first job, and only left because I had the opportunity to move on to a job working with horses, which was the job I really wanted.

North to Alaska

Growing up in Bray our main occupation on a Saturday was going to the "pictures", and one of my favourites was John Wayne in "North to Alaska". Not that I was a John Wayne fan, but I loved the whole gold rush, Yukon, and Alaska theme. When I decided to do the Rocky Mountaineer rail trip from Banff to Vancouver, included at the end was a cruise to Alaska – so despite the fact that cruising would never have been on my agenda I could not resist the lure of going North to Alaska.

The Rocky Mountaineer journey was an incredible experience, but that story is for another day! So up early for a swim in the hotel pool and on to breakfast with the rest of the group, and then at 12 o'clock we gathered in the hall and our luggage was loaded onto a coach which took us all to the dock – a drive of five minutes. Through very strict passport control and checking in and onto the ship, where each of us was greeted by a staff member who escorted you to your cabin. It was one heck of a walk down to Cabin 3006 and it made you realise that you were really on a floating town. Over 1,000 passengers and crew. What surprised me was the range of age groups from children to the very elderly.

There were two days very pleasant sailing through the Northwest Passage, the weather at this point was very pleasant and quite warm but we had been warned that it would get colder the further North we went. Our first port of call was Sitka. My impression of it was that it looked like a cleaned-up mining town, wooden walkways, wooden shop fronts. Sitka was the capital of Russian America when the Russia laid claim to Alaska and the Russian influence was very obvious. There was a Russian Orthodox Church with the usual onion shaped dome.

The next morning was notably chillier, and it was announced that we would be arriving at the Hubbard glacier at about 11.30am and the best place to view was up on Deck 10. We were warned to get well wrapped up. Up we went and the first thing you notice was that the ship had come to a standstill, and there was the most breath-taking sight. Great cliffs of blue ice striated with black moraines. The glacier and icefields stretched back as far as the eye could see. One of the most noticeable things was the noise, the grinding and cracking sounds from the glacier. Then there was and almighty crack and a huge chunk of the face of the cliff crashed into the sea which was scattered with huge lumps of ice. We saw the body of a whale encased in an ice lump moving across the water a really amazing sight.

The staff arrived up on deck with hot chocolate laced with Baileys, and we were really grateful for it as it was absolutely freezing, so you sit with your hands wrapped round the hot mug and drink in one of the most amazing sights in the world.

Juneau was our next port of call, and it was here that we could go whale watching, so it was an early start. Again, Juneau is like the typical Wild West town, at least round the docks area, although they have a university and schools and all the normal trappings of a town. However, it is so isolated and once the cruise ships stop for the season everything closes down and all those working in the tourist industries go home.

The coach set off in pouring rain and drove out along the bay and passed over a number of rivers along the shoreline and we saw a sight that has stayed with me. All along the riverbeds were hundreds of dead salmon. It was the middle of the spawning season, but it was quite upsetting to see all the dying fish, even though you knew the reason, you could also see salmon still jumping the rapids in the river.

We boarded a very comfortable boat which had an upper and lower deck, so we made ourselves comfortable with a nice cup of coffee and then set sail to where the whales were. When we got to the whaling grounds we sat waiting and suddenly there was a shout and we saw a spout from a blow hole and the next thing the back appeared as he dived. Kept seeing random sightings and one great one where we had a perfect sight of the tail disappearing at the end of the dive.

It was still pouring rain, apparently it rains in Alaska for 260 days a year, so we left the outside deck and were sitting at a table by the window and the most incredible thing happened. We saw three whales get in a straight line across and they swan straight at the boat. Some people were getting quite apprehensive as they got nearer and nearer and then dived in unison right under the boat and up the other side. It was so exciting particularly as they did it another four times back and forward under the boat. The guide told us that we were the lucky boat of the day. Apparently, these whales are well known. The leader is called Spot because of the distinctive while spot under his tail, and love playing to the crowd, and they pick a boat and put on their show. It was one of the most memorable experiences I have ever had.

When we got back to Juneau I met up with our guide and we went for coffee but the only place you could go was The Red Dog Saloon. And it really was a saloon in the accepted sense, complete with swing doors, long bar counter, floor covered with sawdust, moose heads over the bar. In the corner was a guy playing a honky tonk piano, wearing a waist coat and bowler hat. He was doing a running commentary, he said "You know I find it amazing that people would spend their holidays in a place where it rains 260 days of the year, not very bright you boat people", but all said with a great sense of fun.

We had been warned that we definitely should not be late back to the ship, as if it went without us there was no other way out of Alaska, no superhighways and just small planes flying out.

The next day we were heading back to Vancouver which was fairly straight forward sailing. However, there is always plenty to do on board, lectures, movies, classes, bridge games, no need to ever be bored. As we sailed home, we saw sightings of whales in the distance, and dolphins but nothing would compare with what we had seen on our way to Alaska. A really memorable holiday.

Thanks for the Memories

For anyone who studied or worked in Dublin in the 50's or 60's, Bewley's on Grafton Street was a familiar stomping ground. A place to meet friends or occasionally a hiding place while on the 'mitch' from secretarial college. No matter how many new places opened, Bewley's was the one constant, mainly because of its down to earth wholesome menu, ambiance but also because of its affordability. One could nearly always scrape up enough for beans and toast.

I was delighted when I got my first job in Dame Street, as this meant I could still use Bewley's for lunch. I always found it fascinating to see the same faces, day after day in Grafton Street until you actually felt you know these people. In fact, many years later when I worked in a hotel in Kerry, I bumped into a woman in the hallway and greeted her like a long-lost friend, only to realise she was one of the Graton Street faces.

Sadly, Bewley's has had to close its doors this year. A sad loss to Grafton Street and Dublin but thanks for the memories.

The Gift

Gifts are often personal, but there are gifts that are unusual, and one of these is Music.

This was brought home to me a couple of weeks ago when watching a programme called "The Greatest Dancer" – a dance competition for groups or individuals.

One of the competitors was a young boy with Downs Syndrome who arrived at the venue with his Mum. He was tall and lumbered awkwardly into the studio room. Watching as his Mum smiled encouragingly at him, I felt this was going to be difficult to watch.

The music started and the transformation was amazing! The awkward stance disappeared, and he became lost in the music. His movements became beautifully fluid, and he brought the audience to their feet.

When the music stopped, he was once again the awkward young man who had walked into the room.

To me, music was a gift to him which for a short while opens a different world to him. Luckily, he is not the only one to whom music would be seen as a gift - a gift that can transport a person to another place, time or moment and lifts your soul.

We all have gifts, it could be the ability to write, to sing, to teach, to be kind the gifts are endless, we just have to find our own.

The Great Wall

We were up very early to make our way to the Great Wall. The excitement at breakfast was palpable. We got on a coach to be driven through Beijing to the central station. It was our first experience of this unbelievable city. The main impression was of people, people, and more people even though it was 6.30 in the morning. The traffic had to be seen to be believed. Thousands of bicycles, rickshaws, horses and carts, buses, coaches, every form of transport imaginable. On the wide pavements thronged with people, we saw people out walking their birds in bamboo cages. Apparently, this is a status symbol. You are a one bird person or a two-bird person or the highest status of all, a three-bird person and this is because you have to hire a person to carry the third cage.

We arrived at the station, again thousands of people rushing to and from trains. What strikes you is the constant sound of humanity on the move. A background noise which rises and falls all the time. We board our train which is surprisingly comfortable. Chinese tea is served in typical Chinese cups and the delicate smell of the tea still stays with me and I will always associate that smell with trains. As we sipped our tea, we watched the landscape passing by. Acres and acres of green flat land which was being farmed with corn or rice. Again, so many people working, planting, gathering, nonstop activity but all with an impression of tranquillity.

We arrive at Badaling, the station for the Great Wall and ten on a coach to drive to one of the entrances to the Great Wall. How can one describe it! Everyone has read about it, seen it on television and film, even seen it as it is from space but to climb it is another thing entirely. And you literally climb it. It runs straight up the spine of the mountain and then disappears as it goes down the other side. You can see it wind on up and down the mountain into the far distance.

We struggled up the vertical in front of us. The surface looks like great slabs of slate. They say you could hide five horses abreast on it, but I think they must have been very small horses. The surface looks as if it would be very treacherous in snow or rain. We continued to climb and eventually came to the crest, and we decided to stop there. It was quite extraordinary to stand there and look out across the Mongolian plains on one side and China on the other. You could feel the sense of history, see Genghis Khan and his hordes galloping across the plains and pulling up short at the sight of the insurmountable obstacle. If you stood still the noise of all those walking the wall, and there was a non-stop flow, seemed to recede and in your mind, you could hear the horses' hooves and the jingle of the harnesses, as the sentries patrolled the wall.

The spell broken, we turn and head back down. As we went, we passed a Chinese family on the way up, which included on very old lady who had the tiniest feet I have ever seen, and the guide told us later that it was a result of the binding of feet which was practised in China up until quite recently.

The journey home on the coach was very subdued as everyone was contemplating the experience we had just had. Unforgettable!

The Kitten Who Fell on her Feet

"Where am I" thought the little ginger kitten. Everything had happened so quickly, one minute she was playing happily with her brother and sister and the next thing she knew she had been bundled into a box. She heard the lady's voice saying, "we have homes for the others, but this one will have to go to the vet". "What was a vet?" thought the ginger kitten. Although she was quite frightened, she consoled herself thinking perhaps the vet is something nice, and it will be a lovely surprise.

Next thing she heard a door slam and suddenly there was a humming sound and she felt movement. She really was very frightened all alone in the dark, being bumped up and down, and she really missed her brother and sister and wished they were here with her. Suddenly the movement stopped, and she heard a door opening and felt the box being lifted. She heard voices and then the lid was opened, and the box flooded with light. She could hardly see a thing having been in the dark for so long. Big gentle hands lifted her from the box, and a nice voice said "Well, this is a pretty one, we should have no trouble getting a home for her. We'll just pop her in the cage and hopefully someone will come along and give her a home". "But I have a home" thought the little kitten, and then she realised the man who had brought her was packing the box and leaving – without her, she was being left in this place away from her mother and brother and sister, and she might never see them again. She threw herself against the bars of the cage in a frantic attempt to get out and follow the man back to what she had thought of as her home. "There, there" said the nice voice, "don't get yourself upset, just settle down". How could she settle down? Her world had turned upside down – what was she to do?

She prowled round and round the cage, meowing frantically and suddenly a very gruff voice said, "For goodness sake stop that prowling around and making that noise, you're making me dizzy and deaf". The little kitten was startled, she hadn't really looked around her, and now in the dim light she could make out other cages. The voice had come from the cage beside her, and she saw that it was occupied by a rather scruffy dog with a face that looked like it had come through many a rough and tumble. "What's wrong with you" he demanded. "I miss my brothers and sisters, I've been left here all on my own, I just don't understand what's happening". "Oh, that's easy", said the scruffy dog, "they didn't want you, so they've left you here in the hope that someone will give you a home". The little kitten was so upset, "why did they not want me" she said, "I was a good little kitten, I never messed, I kept out of the way, I did all the things I was supposed to, not like my brother who was always in trouble". "They just didn't have room for you, count yourself lucky, they could have had you put down". At this the little kitten burst into tears, "what was being put down", she thought, she didn't like the sound of it one little bit. Put down where, for goodness sake! She really was most confused and upset so she rolled herself up into a ball in the corner of her cage and squeezed her eyes tight shut. This didn't stop the tears from coming, and eventually she cried herself to sleep.

She woke with a start, what was that noise? Then she realised where she was, and a wave of sadness broke over her again. She saw a girl in a white coat opening and shutting the doors of the cages and putting in dishes of what looked like food. It was only then that she realised just how hungry she was. Suddenly it was her turn, and the girl opened the cage and looked in. "You're new", she said, "and what a pretty kitten you are, what a lovely colour. We'll have to look for a really nice home for you. Now, here's some breakfast, I'm sure you're hungry". She patted the little kitten and put down the dish with food and milk. The little kitten ate up everything and drank up all the milk. Then she sat down to have a good wash, just like her mother had taught her.

After she had washed, she began to look around her, and saw her gruff companion of the previous night in the next cage, and curiosity began to get the better of her, and she said, "Good morning, may I ask if you are here looking for a home as well". "I most certainly am not, I have a very loving home, my family think the world of me. Unfortunately, I got into a fight and had to have stitches in my leg" he said. "Do you get into many fights," said the little kitten. "Quite a few" he admitted, "but I usually win. By the way, my name is Scruffy. Look here, I'm sorry if I upset you last night, I shouldn't worry about getting a home, after all look at me, this is where I started out and I got a lovely home. And let's face it I'm not nearly as pretty as you. This is a big town and there are lots of families looking for pets, so cheer up". The little kitten felt much better after that. The sun was shining in the window into the corner of her cage, and she curled up in the warmth and decided to have another snooze.

She was fast asleep when she was awakened by the sound of voices, she heard a man's voice say "Yesterday her dog was savaged by a guard dog and killed, so we thought we would like to come and see what animals you have. We know we can't replace Brutus, but we could give another animal a good home". There was a little girl with the man, and he said "Well, Janice, will we have a look and see", and the little girl started to look in the cages. The little kitten jumped up and tried to make herself as pretty as possible, she rubbed up against the front of the cage, and stood on her hind legs and rattled the cage door to try to attract the little girl's attention, but her cage was right at the end of the row and she was really getting worried that the little girl would choose before she got to her. "Please, Scruffy, what can I do to get them to look at me, can you kick up a row or something and get them down this end before she sees someone else". "Sure thing", said Scruffy, and he threw back his head and let out the most blood curdling yell, that really frightened the little kitten. Then she heard the man's voice outside Scruffy's cage saying, "Well, you're a rowdy one, and been in a scrap by the look of it". Scruffy moved over to the side of the kitten's cage, and then the kitten heard the man say, "Look, Janice, see what's down here, we nearly missed it, isn't it a lovely kitten. I know you'd like a dog but what do you think of this little mite?" The little girl's face lit up with a smile as she looked at the kitten, and as the kitten looked back at her they both knew it was love at first sight. "No, Daddy, I don't want another dog, I want this kitten. This is what I really want". The girl in the white coat came along and opened the cage, and the kitten just had time to say, "Thank you, Scruffy", when she was whisked out of the cage and handed to the little girl. "Best of luck, little one", shouted Scruffy, "we may meet again sometime".

Then everything seemed to happen at once, the vet asked if he would give them a box for the kitten to travel in and the little girl said, "Oh no, I'll wrap her in this cardigan and hold her in the car on my lap". "Well, hold her tight" said the girl in the white coat, "you don't want her to run away". "Run away! No way", thought the little kitten, "I've found my home and I know I'm going to be happy there with Janice and the nice man". Then it was into the car and off on the journey to my new home.

It didn't take too long until the car stopped, and the nice man got out and came round and helped Janice out of the car. "Carefully does it", he said "don't want to drop her, the first thing we are going to have to do is pick a name for her. Let's get inside and show everyone what we've brought home". The little kitten just had time to wonder who everyone was when the door opened, and she got the first sight of her new home and family. There was a tall lady with dark hair and two other little girls, and they were all crowding around. "Give her a chance", laughed the man, "you'll have her squashed if you're not careful". Janice then put the cardigan on the kitchen table, and everyone looked with delight at the little ball of ginger fur on the table. There was great excitement and the other little girls wanted to pick up the little kitten, but the lady said, "Let's give her a chance to look around and get her bearings before we start picking her up, it must all be very strange to the poor little thing". "Strange it may be", thought the little kitten, "but it won't be strange for long, this is my new home", and she jumped in the air with excitement. Everyone laughed and the smallest of the girls picked her up and cuddled her.

"Now", said Janice, "the most important part, a name". Well, there were all sorts of suggestions and then someone said that perhaps because the kitten was such a lovely colour that it should be something to do with that. There were all sorts of suggestions – Ginger, Red, Marmalade, and then someone said what about Amber, and everyone agreed that should be the little kitten's name. The little kitten kept repeating the name to herself and the more she said it the more she liked it. The three girls then set about giving Amber here first meal in her new home and Amber realised she was hungry again, so she tucked in, and then with a full tummy she jumped on Janice's knee, and fell fast asleep, safe in the knowledge that she had a new home and a family that loved her, and she was looking forward to to-morrow, and the adventures it would bring.

A New Life

Amber woke the next morning to find herself in a big roomy basket with a soft pillow which she had snuggled into. She didn't remember being put into it; all the excitement of the previous few days must have made her very tired. Her bed was beside a range which glowed red and gave out a lovely warm feeling. She felt like settling down again but curiosity got the better of her and after a big stretch, she hopped out of the basket and set off to explore here new surroundings. Amber realised she was in the kitchen as she could see the sink and the cooker, and then in the corner was a huge square shaped box which made a gentle humming noise, which Amber thought was very familiar. Cautiously Amber crept towards it, and right down at the ground there was a lovely red light, she went toward the red light and the humming noise got a little louder. Amber sat down and looked at this box like thing but could not decide what it was so she went a little closer and sat beside the red light she could feel a slight tremor from the box, and suddenly she became very homesick, she knew now what the noise reminded her of, it was like her Mother's purring when she would lie down with Amber and her brothers and sister, and they would all snuggled in close to her to be lulled to sleep by the lovely purring noise.

Amber wondered sadly how here brothers and sisters were, and most of all did her mother miss her.

Just then the door opened and the tall lady came in, saying "Hurry up, girls it's time for breakfast", and then she turned round and scooped Amber up and said "Hello, little one you're up early, how about some breakfast for you, and after breakfast I must introduce you to Princess, we thought we'd give you a little time to settle before the two of you met". This sounded very exciting, maybe it was another cat. Amber ate up all her breakfast and the three little girls arrived, Janice picked Amber up and gave her a cuddle, and put her on her knee while she ate her breakfast. Then Ciara who was the smallest of the girls asked if she could hold her, so Amber sat on her knee for a while, and then the other little girl, Cliona, said she would like to hold me for a while. This was great fun going from one knee to the other, and Amber was really enjoying herself. "Mum", said Janice, "will we introduce Amber to Princess now before we got to school". "That's a good idea" said Mum, "just go and get Dad and he will bring her in".

The nice man then came into the room and with him he had – not a cat – but a dog! Instinctively Amber drew herself up to her full height, which wasn't very much anyway, and her fur stood on end. Even though she was only a kitten she knew instinctively that cats and dogs didn't really get on, and she would have to defend herself. It wasn't a very big dog, and Dad said, "There we are, you two will have to get to know one another, if you're to live in the same house, and learn to get along". "I don't think so", said Amber, "this is going to be my house". "That's not very nice", said a soft voice, "after all I'm already here, this is my home and has been for the last two years, so I think you should be nice to me". "Oh yea," said Amber acting tough like she had seen her brother do. "Oh, yea" replied the soft but extremely determined voice, "we can do this reasonably or there are other ways, and I don't think you'd like them, so I think we should work things out". Amber looked at Princess and saw the same look on her face that her mother had when she was making sure they did what they were told. Amber couldn't give in straight away, so she gave a hiss and said in a brave voice, "Just keep out of my way and things will be alright". She jumped up on one of the chairs and sat down. "There", said Dad, "that wasn't so bad, I think they will get along fine, you all head off to school and I'll keep an eye on them while I have my breakfast, and make sure there is no trouble". When Dad had finished his breakfast, he got up and said, "Well, I'm off to work now, and I'm going to leave you two to get better acquainted. Princess, old girl, I'm looking to you to look after this little lady and make her welcome like poor Brutus made you welcome when you came", and with that he put on his coat and went out the door.

Princess sat in front of the range and looked at Amber sitting on the chair. "Well,", she said, "it looks like we are just going to have to get along. I'll do anything Dad says, 'cause he is really kind and good, so if he says I'm to make you welcome I'll do so, but how do you feel about it". "I don't know what to feel", said Amber "I always thought cats and dogs just didn't get on, but I have to say I'd much rather be friends than enemies. I really miss my mother most dreadfully, and my brother and sister so it would be nice to have a friend – even if it is a dog". Princess gave a little chuckle and said "OK, friends it is, now how about we have a bit of a snooze in front this nice warm fire and then I will take you to explore the house. You can even snuggle up beside me if you like, and then maybe you won't miss your mother so much". So, Amber jumped down off the chair and came over to where Princess was lying and snuggled up beside her. Princess gently put a paw across the little kitten and drew her in closer and said, "I think we're going to be really good friends you and I". "Oh" said

Amber, looking at Princess's paw which was across her, we're the same colour you and I, what sort of a dog are you anyway?". "I'm a Corgi" said Princess proudly, "that's a very important breed, and I have an extremely good pedigree, my parents are show champions". "What's a pedigree?" asked Amber, and Princess said, "You do ask a lot of questions, and I'm getting very sleepy, so I'll tell you later". And Amber snuggled in against Princess, and she didn't feel lonely anymore. "I am lucky, I've got a lovely new home, a family and now a special friend, I'm sure my mother would be very happy if she knew", and she drifted off to sleep.

"Well, well", said Mum, "you two are certainly getting on well". Princess jumped up and Amber, who had been lying on her tummy shot into the air and turned head over heels before landing on her four paws. "It's a good job cats always land on their feet", she said crossly, "or I would have been in trouble, did you have to jump up so suddenly?". "Sorry", said Princess, "but I always like to make a big fuss when any of the family come home, they all love to get a nice welcome". "Does that mean you're going to jump around the place when anyone comes, if so, I think I will keep out of your way". The lady was laughing at Princess and rubbing her tummy, "You are a good girl, it's always so nice to come home to your welcome. So, you've been looking after Amber, that's good because she really is so small". "I may be small now", said Amber rubbing up against Mum's leg, "but I won't take long to grow up and then I'll nearly be as big as you, Princess". Princess looked at the little kitten, and smiled, and she didn't like to disillusion Amber – cats didn't really grow as big as dogs. "She really doesn't know much about anything, "thought Princess, "I can see I have a lot of teaching to do". "Later on," said Mum "when the girls come home, I will take you out into the garden, that will be a big adventure for you, but it is important you get to know your surroundings, we don't want you getting lost, now do we?" Mum started to do the washing up and Princess said, "Come on you, I'll show you the rest of the house". They set off down the hall towards the front door, "this is what's called a bungalow, there is no upstairs. Now on the right is Mum and Dad's bedroom – we're not allowed in there". "Why not," said Amber. I don't know" replied Princess, "all I know is it is not allowed". "We'll see about that" thought Amber, but she didn't say anything to Princess. "This is the drawing room here, continued Princess, "and at night they build a lovely big fire and when the girls have had their tea and done their homework, they all sit in here, and it is really cosy. The next room is the office. Mum in involved in a thing called the riding clubs and this is where she does all her typing and phone calls and Dad does his business calls in here in the evenings. The girls do their study in here too". Amber jumped up on the table and started to explore. "Come down here" said Princess, "you'll get into trouble". "Why" said Amber. Her eyes were as big as saucers as she saw all the interesting things there. She jumped up on a shelf above the table and suddenly there was an almighty crash, and a holder full of pens and pencils hit the floor. "Now you've done it", said Princess, and Amber who had got quite a shock shot up the curtains and hung there meowing with fright. Mum came rushing into the room to see what all the commotion was about and burst out laughing when she saw Amber hanging on for dear life to the curtains. "Well now, what are you up to, you little scamp", she said "it hasn't taken you long to settle in, down you come now, and I'll clear up this mess".

When Amber was down on the floor Princess came over to her and gave her a good box in the ear and said, "you will really have to learn to behave yourself and do what you are told". "Ouch", said Amber, "that hurt". "Serves you right for not coming down when I told you" Princess said as she stamped out of the room.

Amber stayed watching as Mum cleared up the mess, and then scampered after her as she left the room and went back into the kitchen. Mum closed the door and was busy working at the sink when Amber noticed a machine in the corner with a thing like a huge glass eye in the centre of it, and behind the glass she could see things moving round and round in a circle. Amber was fascinated by this and went a bit nearer to get a closer look. Suddenly everything stopped moving and went quiet and just as Amber was about to go nearer, off it went again. Amber felt this definitely needed more examination and she could see that the glass section was sunk back into the machine, so she hopped up on it and realised she was right beside the things that were going round and round, there was only the glass between them. Also, the glass was lovely and warm, and the machine made a throbbing sound. She sat there for quite a while watching and then gradually with the warmth and the noise, she began to feel sleepy, so she lay down where she was against the glass and fell fast asleep.

The next thing she knew was hearing voices talking very quietly and saying, "isn't she funny, look where she has chosen to sleep". "I think she's very clever" Amber heard Janice say, "it's lovely and warm and she's off the floor so she won't get stood on, yes, she's a really clever little kitten, and look she's awake, can I give her something to eat, Mum". So, with Mum's permission Janice got down the food and laid out a bowl of milk ready for Amber, who hopped down and tucked in as she was hungry after her long sleep.

"Now, it's time to show her the garden and get her used to the outside", said Mum, "so when you girls are ready, we'll pop outside with her". The girls pulled on their coats, Janice picked Amber up and Mum opened the door. Just outside the door there were steps and Janice went up these and Amber could not believe her eyes, there was so much to look at. She had never been outside before, and had only seen little bits through the windows, so she found it very hard to take in what she was seeing. "Put her down on the grass" said Mum, and the next thing Amber found herself standing on some green springy stuff which seemed to cover a lot of the garden. She gingerly put one foot in front of the other and then decided this stuff was really nice to walk on, so then she tried a little run, and then a jump and she was really starting to enjoy herself when suddenly out of the corner of her eye she saw something fly across the grass and she turned round and jumped on it pinning it to the ground. "Oh, look", said Janice "she's chasing a leaf". "Well, at this time of the year she'll have no shortage of them to chase", said Mum. Just then another leaf went past, and Amber jumped on that one, and then another, she didn't know which one to run after. One of them spun into the air, and Amber jumped as high as she could but couldn't catch it, then she saw something she could climb up to get higher and she shot up this and heard Janice shout "Oh, look she's gone up the tree". Poor Amber there really was so much to take in, so many new words to learn, she hoped she'd be able to remember them – grass, leaves, tree and now they were talking about the sky, and Amber realised that was the blue thing above them which seems to stretch over everything. Amber saw the leaf she had been chasing further up the tree and she climbed higher, but it just seemed to go higher and higher and she kept climbing and then the leaf shot up into the sky and was blown away. Amber looked around and she could see into the gardens beside theirs, and she looked over the roof of the house and she could see another big stretch of blue with little white bits on it, it seemed to stretch for miles, and then she turned the other way and saw a mountain with a white cross on the top, it was all quite amazing. She heard Janice's voice calling her name and she looked down, and she got such a fright - she was miles up in the air, she dug her claws in the branch and meowed wildly, she didn't know what to do, she couldn't move, she was so afraid she was shaking all over, so she just hung on and closed her eyes. She didn't know how long she was there, but suddenly she heard Dad's voice quite close to her and then she felt a hand go around her, she was still afraid to let go but he said, "Come on, little one, I've come to take you back down, you've certainly got yourself up high enough", so Amber let go and the next thing Dad tucked her inside his jumper and climbed down out of the tree. The girls made a great fuss of her, and even Princess joined in. Then they all went into the house for tea.

Later on, that evening when Princess and Amber settled down for the night, Princess asked if Amber was feeling O.K. "I am now" said Amber, "but I was so frightened up that tree. It was fine until I looked down, and then I just didn't know what to do". "Well, the next time we go outside", said Princess "I'll show you how to climb up and get down again, if you like. The secret is in the beginning not to go up too high and learn how to get down from the lower branches first, and then when you've practiced you can go higher". "Thank you", said Amber gratefully "I really wouldn't like to be that frightened ever again. Can I ask you something though? When I was up the tree, I looked over the house and I saw a whole lot of blue stuff with little white patches, what was that, it looked huge". "Oh", said Princess "that's the sea. Now, that is really fun stuff. The girls take me across there to swim". "Ugh" said Amber, "you mean its water, I hate water. I certainly won't be going over there, thank you very much! Is there anything else out there"? "There certainly is, the whole world is out there" said Princess "it's called the Seafront and beside us there are the amusements where people go to have fun and ride on things called the bumpers and merry go-rounds and the Ghost Train. There are lots of ice cream shops, and fish and chip shops, and in the summer crowds and crowds of people come out to swim, and sit in the sun on the beach, and have picnics, and further up the beach there is a fun fair. It really is exciting, but you have to be careful when you go out there because there are lots of cars, and sometimes you find people who are not that nice to animals, so you have to watch yourself. One day I'll take you out to the front wall and you can sit on it and have a look for yourself, but please, Amber, don't go wandering off". "Alright", said Amber meekly, too meekly thought Princess, who realised that the little kitten had had a really bad fright and for the moment was prepared to do what she was told, but how long would that last. Then they both curled up in their respective beds, and Princess was just about to go to sleep when she felt Amber climb into her bed and curl up beside her. Princess stretched out a paw and pulled her in close, she licked her head gently and very soon there wasn't a sound in the kitchen but the gentle breathing of two contented animals.

Over the next few weeks Amber really thrived and grew steadily. Thanks to Princess she learnt all sorts of survival techniques, and now could go to the very top of the tree and back down again without any bother. By now she was allowed out in the garden on her own and one day she decided it was time she explored the garden next door, so she found a place in the hedge where she could just about squeeze through. The garden was different than hers, firstly it had no trees, just grass and that was very long, and Amber had to push her way through. Suddenly she heard a noise quite close, so she flattened down the way Princess had taught her and lay very, very still. The noise seemed to be getting closer and was now very loud and the grass in front of Amber started to tremble, poor Amber she didn't know whether to try to run for it or just stay still in the hope that whatever it was would go past. Then the grass in front of Amber parted and a very gravelly voice said, "And what do we have here, and where did you spring from". Amber was speechless, she had never seen anything like it – it was a talking rock, well not quite, because it had a head and neck sticking out the side, and it had two small black eyes that started unblinkingly at Amber. "Speak up can't you, I asked you a question". "I'm sorry" spluttered Amber, "you….you surprised me, I thought I was on my own and then you appeared, and ……………….," "What's wrong – cat got your tongue", and at that the moving rock started to laugh, at least Amber thought it was a laugh, it sounded like a whole lot of stones rubbing together, "That's a joke", it said, "clever or what?" "Oh, yes" said Amber "very clever". She was feeling a little braver now as the moving rock didn't seem to be going to attack her or anything. "Now" it said, "answer my question". "I live next door", said Amber, "I'm a cat and my name is Amber". "I know you're a cat, I'm not stupid or blind – so you live next door now with that rowdy pompous dog". "She's not rowdy or pom..pom..whatever" said Amber indignantly. "Huh", said the rock "I've already had words with her and told her not to try to come into this garden, that she wouldn't be welcome, we tortoises don't like dogs, because sometimes they roll us over on our backs and we can't get upright again, and that is very serious and we can even die, and she said I needn't get so hoity toity as she had a lovely garden of her own and she was a very important breed of dog and didn't mix with the likes of tortoises and had better things to do with her time, and stamped off with her head in the air as if she was royalty". "So that's what you're called" said Amber "a tortoise". "Of course," retorted the tortoise, "really you are very ignorant, what did you think I was?" "I thought you were a talking rock", said Amber feeling a bit ashamed. "Oh that's alright", said the tortoise "it's an easy mistake, watch this" and he pulled his head and neck inside his shell, and he looked exactly like a rock. Amber laughed with delight and said "That's brilliant, do it again" so the tortoise obligingly did it again. "What's your name?" said Amber. "Joe Loss", said the tortoise, "I was named after a famous band leader, actually I was called Dead Loss in the beginning, but then my family decided that wasn't very nice and changed it. I've been here ever so long because you see tortoises live for a very long time. Actually, it is coming into Winter now and I am just looking for somewhere to dig myself in so that I can go to sleep for the whole Winter, it's called hibernation". Amber had never heard so many big words, she thought the tortoise must be very wise. "Does that mean I won't be able to come and visit your" "'Fraid so," said Joe Loss, "but never mind in the Spring we'll be able to get together again, and you can tell me all about what you've done for the Winter, and by then you'll be quite grown up". Just then Amber heard Janice calling from next door, and she said to her new friend, "I hope you find a nice place to hiber...... whatever and I will see you in the Spring" and she ran off to find the hole in the hedge, she squeezed through and hurled herself off the top step into Janice's arms. "Hello, you", said Janice "have you had an exciting day, you really are getting adventurous". That night when Amber and Princess went to bed Amber told Princess all about her adventures next door. Princess snorted when she heard what the tortoise had said about her and said that compared to the tortoise, she certainly was royalty, and Amber just smiled and snuggled down to sleep.

Some weeks later Amber noticed that the weather was getting much colder, and Princess explained that this was what was called Winter, and it would get even colder, and it would get dark much earlier in the evenings and would be dark in the mornings. Amber didn't understand this, and she just accepted it as something else she had learnt.

One day when the girls were at school Mum went out the front to put some stuff in the car and left the door open, and Amber just couldn't resist it, she dashed out the door and hid under the hedge which ran along the wall. Mum came back and went into the house and then came out again and went out the front gate and got into the car and drove off. "Now I've done it", thought Amber, "I've no way of getting back in until someone comes home. Oh well, I'll just have to get all my exploring in before then". Amber walked down the garden to the front wall which had a little white rail along the top, it was a big wide wall, so she sat down behind the rail and looked out. There was a very wide roadway and then a big step up to what looked like a walkway, and then Amber remembered Princess talking about the prom and people walking along it beside the sea, and it was then that Amber realised where the very loud noise she could hear was coming from. It was beyond the walkway, and she knew that it was the sea. Princess had described how when the sea was rough the big waves came in and crashed down on the beach, and if the tide was really high how they would even spill over onto the road and come as far as the front gate. "I hope it's not high tide now", thought Amber, "particularly as I have no way of getting into the house again". Anyway, she sat there and watched everything that was going on outside the railings. She could see the amusements that Princess had spoken about, but they were all closed because it was this thing called Winter and so cold. There were a few people walking along with their dogs, and a few people walked right past the wall that Amber was sitting on, and one nice lady even stopped and spoke to her and petted her.

Suddenly she heard a noise off to the right and realised it was two dogs fighting, then she saw a man on the prom calling to the dogs and the fight broke off and one of the dogs ran up to the man and went off with him.

The other dog walked along in front of the wall, he didn't see Amber and she stayed very quiet as she did not want to attract his attention, even with the railing she wasn't sure that he couldn't get at her. But just as he passed underneath her, she let out a shriek of delight, "Scruffy, Scruffy, it's you, isn't it?" "What's that, who's that" the familiar gruff voice said. "Scruffy, it's me, don't you remember me from the vets, you helped me get my family". "Well, I never" said Scruffy "it's the little ginger one, so this is where you live, you've done well for yourself, and right beside the sea". "I don't like the sea," said Amber. "Of course," said Scruffy "you're a cat". "I see you're still getting into fights," said Amber. "'Fraid so" said Scruffy, "I just can't resist a good punch up, I know I shouldn't but it's so much fun. Actually, I should be home by now, I'm not really supposed to come out on my own but I got bored so I thought I'd nip out and see if I could find anything exciting going on. I don't live too far from here, so I come down the seafront – that's where most of the action is. Anyway, tell me about your family". So, Amber proceeded to tell Scruffy everything about the family, and then she told him about Princess. Scruffy's ears pricked up at this and Amber quickly said "No, Scruffy, you cannot fight with Princess". "Oh, I wasn't thinking of fighting with her, she's a lady, I don't fight with lady dogs – and from what you tell me she sounds like a true lady, you must introduce us". "I'd like to" said Amber, "but you would have to promise to behave like a gentleman, she is actually out with Mum in the car at the moment so it will have to be some other time". "That's OK", said Scruffy, "next time I'm down here I'll look out for you and then you can introduce me, but I must go now and get home, see you soon, Amber" and off he went down the road and round the corner out of sight.

Just as Scruffy disappeared Amber saw the car coming down the road and so she ran to the front door and hid behind a plant pot. Once the door was opened, she slipped in and ran into the kitchen. She was safe and sound again and no one knew of her adventure.

The Taj Mahal

The segregated queues snake to the turnstiles
Indians on the left, foreigners to the right
The dust, the heat, the noise come in waves.
The throbbing essence that is India

Beyond the turnstiles they mingle
Like a sea of noise and colour
Flowing through the harem's gardens
Towards the first glimpse of what all have come to see

And suddenly framed in the massive gateway there it is
In all its glory
Shah Jahan's legacy to the world
Oh, how he must have loved her, his beautiful Mumtaz
Mahal
To build this monument to her memory and to his
broken heart

The sounds of the crowd recede from my consciousness
I stand as if alone, breathless before its beauty
The white marble, tinged pink shimmers in the fierce
Indian sun
It is a moment frozen in time that I will never forget

The Umbrella

Judith looked round the attic and gave a sigh of relief. "Thank goodness", she said to her friend, Penny. "I thought it would be crammed with stuff but there's only this old-fashioned travel trunk". Judith and her friend Penny were clearing out Judith's grandmother's house following her death, and this was the last area to clear. They struggled down the attic steps with the trunk and when they got it to the landing, they opened it up and to their surprise there were just two items in it. A beautiful inlaid jewellery box and what looked like a bundle of sticks. They lifted the two items out, and after examining the bundle of sticks realised that there was more to it than that. After much manipulation, they realised that it opened up and became what looked like an umbrella. It was made of very stiff material nearly like leather in texture and it was decorated with pictures of animals, trees, and flowers. It was quite fascinating but both girls were at a loss as to what exactly it was. So on to Mr Google to see if they could find out anything about it. They were amazed at the amount of information there was about umbrellas, but it looked like what they had was described as a parasol used in Egypt by the very wealthy to keep them sheltered from the ferocious sun.

"This is really interesting but what on earth am I going to do with it," said Judith. Penny turned to her and opening her handbag she showed Judith a leaflet from her bag. It was an advert for the Antiques Roadshow which was coming to Eggmount Castle the next day. "Let's go and take it with us and see if they can help us". The following morning the girls were up early and headed for the Castle. Despite being so early there was already quite a queue. They joined the queue, and a researcher came and asked the girls what they had brough and then allocated them to an expert.

The expectation of the crowd was palpable when the group of experts arrived. "I hope that's our expert", Judith said pointing to a very attractive, dark haired young man. "I could fancy him". As it turned out this was their expert, Harvey Johnson and soon it was their turn. Judith placed the umbrella on the table in front of him, saying "I'm not 100% sure what this actually is, but…"

"Not to worry" he replied with a smile, "that's what I'm here for".. He slowly opened the umbrella and certainly seemed to be fascinated by it. "Can you tell me what you know about it".

"Not a lot", Judith said. I found it in my grandmother's attic when I was cleaning her house, so I have no idea where it came from".

"Well, I think I do" Harvey said "and I think it's quite a story. This umbrella is very old. It came from Egypt originally, and it was brought back to England by a soldier from London who fought in that campaign. He brough it home as a present for his girlfriend. Then he was sent overseas again and when he came home, he found his girlfriend's house had been destroyed in the blitz and the no one was sure if the family had survived. Someone said they thought maybe the daughter had but no one was sure, and there were no records. He searched as best he could and for a long time but no luck and eventually, he had to accept that he had lost her. And now you have brought this here and I recognised it from a photo my uncle always kept of the love of his live posing with this very umbrella. I'm sure if I show it to you, you will recognise your grandmother.

Judith and Penny were absolutely speechless. What an amazing story and an amazing coincidence. "Can I leave the valuation to another time, maybe after we meet up and I show you the photo. What do you think?"

"I think that would be fine", Judith said. She was thinking not only will we resolve the story, but I get to meet the gorgeous Harvey again. Her grandmother was certainly looking down on her.

The Waiting Room

Laura stood in the kitchen drinking a cup of tea, as she waited for Mrs Frame to come in from the calving shed to give her a lift to the station. She had enjoyed her work placement with the Frames. It had been hard work as they were at the height of the calving season, but she had learnt so much and was now heading back to college.

Mrs Frame rushed in the door saying "Good, you are ready. We'll head off right away and be in good time for the train. I'm afraid I won't be able to wait with you, as I think there's a bit of a crisis building up with that young cow but there is a nice waiting room with a good fire, so the wait won't be too long".

Mrs Frame dropped Laura at the door of the tiny station in the village. It looked more like a house rather than a station. Laura went through what looked like the front door and found herself in a room which had a hatch in the corner with a sign above saying ticket office. Behind the counter was a small, jolly looking man who gave her a big smile, and said "Welcome, I take it you are off to Dublin on the train?".

"Yes" replied Laura. "Could I have a single to Heuston please".

"That's a really nasty and cold morning out there, so if you'd like to sit in the waiting room, there's a fine big fire and you'll be nice and warm. Don't worry, I'll call for you when the train is coming in". He pointed at the far corner of the room and Laura saw the sign for the waiting room above the door.

Laura opened the door of the waiting room, and it was as the ticket man had described. There was one other person sitting in the room and Laura said good morning and settled down. The lady sitting opposite smiled and said "It's not such a good morning with that weather. Nasty for travelling but at least we're nice and warm here". She went back to reading her magazine and Laura was able to study her. She was dressed very elegantly, if a little old fashioned. She had a most attractive hat and was wearing gloves and a beautiful pair of lace up high heel boots finished off the outfit. Laura wondered where she was going – a wedding, an important lunch, a secret assignation? Laura mentally shook herself, "stop being ridiculous and mind your own business".

"I'm going to the restroom", Laura said to her companion. "If the ticket man comes, can you give me a shout. I don't want to miss the train".

"Of course, dear", she replied.

When Laura came out of the toilets, the woman had gone. "Damn, she didn't call me" thought Laura. She quickly gathered her bag and rushed towards the door, nearly bumping into the ticket man. "I was just coming to say the train will be here in ten minutes".

"Oh" said Laura. "What about the other lady, she on the platform?"

He looked a bit puzzled and said "which other lady? You're the only passenger this morning".

"But she was in the waiting room with me. We spoke".

Laura went on to describe the lady. The ticket man went a little pale. "You've described Lady Vivienne Clarke, and this is the anniversary of her death. It's a tragic story. She was going to Dublin for a reunion with her fiancé and she stepped on ice on the platform and fell in front of the train and was killed. The Story goes that she has been seen around the station on the anniversary, but I never believed it until now".

To Infinity and Beyond

It was a beautiful summer day under a clear blue sky. Tommy, Pat, and Fred sat on the bank of the stream, enjoying the sunshine, and chatting inanely as 12-year-old boys do. Chatting about anything and everything. Suddenly, Tommy lay back looking up at the sky, squinting into the sunshine.

"Have you ever thought of what's up there?" he said.

Pat hooted with laughter and replied, "do you mean heaven?"

"No, I don't mean heaven, I mean the sun, the moon, the stars, the planets".

"Oi, that a bit deep for a conversation on a sunny afternoon," said Fred.

"No, I'm serious," said Tommy. "I think about it a lot, in fact I'm thinking of becoming an astronaut when I leave school".

"A what!" said Pat "do you mean a spaceman?"

"No, I mean a proper astronaut, and I'm going to the moon".

"Yes, you and Buzz Lightyear. To infinity and beyond!" jeered Fred.

Tommy was feeling a bit cross that his friends were making fun of something that he was taking so seriously. Things went from bad to worse when the boys left the stream and joined a large group of friends at the park in the town and Fred and Pat told them that Tommy was going into space. Before he knew it everyone in the school was calling him Lightyear.

Tommy lay back in his co-pilot's seat in the Icarus II rocket on its way to the moon and looked through the porthole at earth. He wondered where Fred and Pat were now, as he went to infinity and beyond!

Trans-Siberian Encounter

It happened on the Trans-Siberian railway. We had settled down for our first evening on the train when a figure appeared in the doorway of our carriage carrying a bottle of vodka. "Hello, I am Yuri, and I would like to welcome you to Russia and to drink with you some real Russian vodka". This little speech was delivered in very heavily accented English.

We called a couple more of the group we were travelling with, and they all piled into the carriage and a vodka party ensued.

Yuri explained haltingly that he had not spoken English for four years, so "my English, no good". He was such an open person all about his life. He was a physicist and lived in Moscow in a small apartment. He told us how much he earned, which really didn't sound an awful lot for his job. He said he had a dacha outside Moscow on a lake where he could grow flowers and vegetables, in fact it was the law. If you did not cultivate the land your dacha was on, it could be taken away from you. He was travelling to collect his daughter who was visiting with her grandmother.

Although he could speak a fair amount of English, he obviously found our accents difficult, so he would ask us to write it down, but would we please tear the papers up when he left. We noticed that he came down to visit late at night when he knew that our Russian guide was in bed. It began to dawn on us that the Russian carriages were segregated from us, and that Yuri should probably not be with us, but we enjoyed his company, and his secret was safe with us.

After three nights we arrived in Omsk where you could get out and stretch your legs but imagine our horror when we saw Yuri being marched down the platform by two soldiers as if he was under arrest.

That evening we sat in trepidation waiting to see if Yuri would appear, and thankfully he did. He told us that he had been reported. We were pretty sure it was Nadia, our local guide, who we were now convinced was KGB. They wanted to know what we were talking about. To put this in context it happened back in 1983 when the Berlin Wall still existed and the cold war was still very chilly, and we were one of the first tourist groups to travel on the Trans-Siberian.

Yuri convinced them that it was just what it was, a completely innocent interaction and they let him go. More vodka all around that night!

Saoirse's Commute

Saoirse stood on the platform at Marden waiting for the 7.30am commuter train to Cannon Street Station. She waved to her friend Maeve who was on the other platform waiting for the train to Ashford where she was working but she didn't get much reaction. Maeve was not a morning person. She and Maeve had left Ireland to experience working and living away from home, and they now shared a house in Marden with two other girls.

The train pulled in on the dot of 7.30am and Saoirse got on and was lucky enough to get a seat at the window. The train was really filling up and by the time it got to Cannon Street it would be standing room only.

Saoirse enjoyed the hour-long commute. She would put in her earbuds and settle down to listen to a podcast on her phone. She loved to people watch as she listened. This morning's podcast listening was Jarlath Regan's "An Irishman Aboard" with Miriam O'Callaghan. Listening to her voice made Saoirse think back to last night's phone call with her mum.

Saoirse had worried when she decided to come and work in London that her mum would be lonely at home in Dalkey, particularly as her brother Jason was doing his internship in Cork University Hospital, so he wasn't home either. Ever since her dad had walked out on them when she was eight years old, she had worried about her mum. Although she seemed to cope quite well and had thrown herself into her work as a surgeon in a busy Dublin hospital and making sure her children didn't want for anything, physically or emotionally.

Because her dad had a job that took him away from home quite a lot, Saoirse hadn't taken much notice when he left. It was only when it got to Christmas that she asked her mum when dad would be home. She would never forget the look on her mum's face when she sat Saoirse and Jason, who was just six, down to explain that dad wouldn't be coming home anymore. He had left them, that she didn't know where he was, and they were on their own now. Saoirse was devastated and couldn't believe that her lovely dad, who always said she was his best girl and that he couldn't believe that he had such a lovely daughter, had left them.

Life gradually settled down into a routine without him, but Saoirse missed him so much and she felt her mum did too though they never discussed it. Saoirse took a photo of her dad out of the family album. She kept it in her wallet, and it had become well-worn over the years.

Her attention was drawn back as she heard the announcement for the next station, Paddock Wood. As she gazed out the window, she saw the tall, dark-haired man, who she had noticed before. She felt sure he was very familiar but couldn't place where she might have seen him before.

The train arrived at Cannon Street, and everyone piled off, rushing in various directions. Saoirse headed towards her offices which were only 10 minutes from the station. She was a project manager in a huge computer systems company call Folio Link. There were over 800 people working in the company and it was an exciting place to work. Saoirse loved her job.

After one particularly hectic day, Saoirse was heading home and she was a little later than usual, so at least she thought the train wouldn't be so crowded. She got a seat by the window and was getting settled when someone took the seat opposite. She looked up to see "Paddock Wood man" sitting opposite her. He smiled and said "this is much better than the morning train, at least I got a seat. I notice you always get a seat, so you obviously get on much earlier than Paddock Wood". Saoirse was surprised he had noticed her, but she said "yes, I get on at Marden, and it starts to fill up from here". "Yes" he said, "it's touch and go if you get a seat after that. By the way, my name is Jason". "Oh, I'm Saoirse. I have a brother called Jason". Jason smiled at her and said, "You're Irish, aren't you? My father is Irish, but he's been here since he was a child". They chatted away and then Saoirse asked him what he did. He said he worked in the research and development department of a big company called Folio Link. Saoirse laughed and said "Now, I know why you looked familiar. I must have seen you at work. I'm a project manager at Folio Link". They talked about work, swapping stories and before they knew it, the announcement came for Paddock Wood.

From then on, Saoirse and Jason met quite often on the train, and even had lunch in the canteen a couple of times. Saoirse was hoping that things might progress further as she really liked him. Jason had suggested they might meet for lunch some Saturday in Marden, but no definite arrangement had been made.

One day, Saoirse felt she needed a break and would go out and get a sandwich from the deli down the street. She was coming out the office door when she saw Jason in front of her. "Hi, Jason," she called, "are you going to lunch?" "I'm actually meeting my dad. He's down from Manchester for the day. In fact, there he is now. I must introduce you". Saoirse turned around and her world spun on its axis. Walking towards her was her father. He looked exactly as he did in her photograph. It dawned on her why Jason had been so familiar. Her half-brother was the image of her father.

The look of shock on his father's face made Jason falter in his introduction, and when he saw that look mirrored on Saoirse's face, he realised something was happening that he didn't understand.

Saoirse was suddenly galvanised into action. She turned on her heel and fled into the crowd. She heard her name being called but there was no way she could face this now. She needed time.

Tsunami

Everyone tells a different story about that event, but this is mine.

I woke early that morning with the sun beaming in the window as it had the previous three days of our holiday. I looked across at the other bed and said "Come on sleepy head, it's another glorious day in Paradise, let's head for the beach. I was greeted with a groan from under the bed covers, "I feel awful, I've been up most of the night getting sick, you just bloody slept through it all" "Oh, Jane, I'm so sorry, I was so tired after all the activity yesterday and then the party I just passed out". "Tell me about it, you could have dropped a bomb on you, and you wouldn't have budged. Look, why don't you go ahead and if and when I feel up to it, I'll follow you down". "Are you sure, can I get you anything before I go"? This was greeted by a groan and "just go away".

When I got downstairs, I went into the dining room and grabbed some fruit and headed straight for the beach, through the gardens and past the pool where the early morning swimmers were already splashing around. I threw my towel and bag on one of the beach beds and ran down to the sea. I paused to look at the beautiful view, the sun sparkling on the azure sea, and the waves lapping gently round my feet. After a lovely leisurely swim, I stretched out on my beach bed and closed my eyes. A few minutes later I heard a bit of a commotion. A young mum was settling on to the bed next to mine. She had a baby in a buggy and a toddler who was shouting with delight as she dug into the sand with a spade. I groaned inwardly but smiled and said "Hi". The young Mum who I had seen in the dining room with her husband and kids said "Hi, I'm Joy, I hope you don't mind me sitting here". "Of course not," I replied, "she looks like she loves the beach". "Yes, may loves messing with the sand". As we were talking, I suddenly got the feeling that something strange was happening, the air seemed to have become very heavy, a really odd feeling, then we heard shouts of excitement, and I looked down towards the sea and couldn't believe my eyes. Where there had been sparkling sea there was nothing except what looked like fish flip flopping on the sand, and people were walking out to look at them.

As a child I had a huge interest in extreme weather conditions and looking at what I saw my senses screamed tsunami. I jumped up and said to Joy" Quickly, pick up the baby. I'll take Amy, we have to get off the beach now. I picked Amy up and said as calmly as possible "we are going to play a game; I'm going to carry you and I want you to put your arms round my neck and hold tight". I tied my sarong round her and myself and tied it tight. "Joy, please hurry we have to get to the hotel we are really in grave danger. Don't worry about the buggy or anything". I screamed at the people near us "Get off the beach now, there's a tsunami coming. Get to higher ground". Many of them looked at me as if I was mad, but I grabbed Joy's hand and started to pull her towards the hotel. The soft sand made it tough going, but eventually we got to the concrete path and started to run towards the hotel. As we ran through the garden I glanced back, and I could see what looked like a black line on the horizon and could hear a sound like the muted roar of a lion. "Oh God, Joy, it's coming, run for your life". Amy seemed to sense what was happening and she tightened her grip round my neck. We flew round the swimming pool and into the hotel lobby. "Get up the stairs quick there is a tsunami coming" I shrieked and yelled at Joy to go to the staircase, we shot through the door to the stairwell and started to climb the stairs. We got to the first floor, then the second floor, others had joined us on the staircase and the feeling of panic filled the air, we reached the fourth Floor, and I could feel my legs getting weaker, the roar of sound was getting louder and louder, as we reached the fifth floor and there was a terrible sound of breaking glass, crashing noises and human screams. I saw the sign for the sixth floor and was pulling myself and Amy up by the banisters, Joy was struggling in front of me. There was an almighty crash and the door at the end of the stairs caved in and I could see the water pouring in and start to swirl up the staircase, picking people up and tossing them around like rag dolls. "Of God, keep going, Joy" I shouted and from somewhere got a spurt of energy, onto the seventh floor and upward we went, suddenly I felt the water round my feet, and thought this is the end. I clung to the banisters as the water reached my waist. Then suddenly there was a change in the roar of sound and the water started to drain away from my body. The sound we heard now was more like the sucking sound you get when emptying the bath and looking back down the stairs we could see the waters receding leaving behind debris and bodies. We could hear the moans and screams of the injured. We were opposite the door onto the 8th floor which was where my room was, so I said to Joy "Let's get my room and get the children safe". I realised when I got to the door that I didn't have the key and I prayed that Jane was ok and still in the room. I banged on the door, and to our relief the door opened and there was Jane looking absolutely terrified "Oh, thank God, you're safe, I saw it all from the balcony, it was unbelievable, I was so sure you were still on the beach". She threw her arms round me, squeezing poor Amy in the process. I staggered over to the bed and unfastened my sarong. "It's ok Amy, you can let go now" I looked down at the little golden-haired toddler and she looked up at me with her big blue eyes and said in a trembling voice "I didn't like that game, I don't want to play it again". I squeezed her tight looking at her Mum over her head and smiled and said "Neither do I, darling, neither do I. Never again".

Unexpected Consequences

Babar sat at Gate 15 waiting to board the flight to Karachi. He could barely contain his excitement. He was finally going home, and he was going to see his beloved mother.

He remembered the day 10 years ago when he had arrived at this very airport – a frightened, bewildered fifteen-year-old. His mother had scrimped and saved, working two jobs, taking in washing.... anything that would make money, to gather the fare to send Babar to London to live with her brother Ahmed, in the hope that he could make a better life. He remembered the tears streaming down her face as she said Goodbye and he felt terrified he wouldn't see her again.

And now here he was heading home. He couldn't wait to surprise his mother. Thanks to his uncle's guidance and his own determination and hard work, he now had a very well-paid job in a Global IT company. He had been sending money home regularly to his mother and he hoped that it had made life easier for her. They didn't have much contact as unfortunately his mother couldn't write and didn't have a phone, so the only news he received was the occasional letter from one of his sisters.

He had forgotten so much about Pakistan, but as he stepped out of the airport at Karachi it came flooding back – the crowds of people, the noise, the hustle and bustle, constant car horns and the smells.

He hailed a taxi and gave the driver the address of his village and asked him to drop him in the square. He walked slowly up the road and saw the familiar house. It looked much smaller than he remembered. He knocked on the door, shaking with excitement.

The door opened and there she was, his beloved Ammi. He saw the shock on her face, followed by joy, but suddenly she clutched her chest and collapsed into his arms. "Oh no, no" he shouted. He looked up and saw his sisters, "Call an Ambulance quickly". He gathered his mother in his arms. Her eyes fluttered open, "My darling Babar, it is you. I love you my darling boy" and she closed her eyes again and sighed.

View from the Train

As far as the eye can see the Russian steppes stretch to the horizon.

The silver branches of the taiga shimmer in the sun.
Along the tracts the pretty wildflowers of Siberia flourish, bright splashes of colour.

Beneath this beauty the permafrost tightens its hold on long forgotten corpses.

The detritus, the cannon fodder of the wars that raged across this land.

Sons, fathers, brothers, uncles lost to their families in the Russian mud.
Sealed to their fates by the fierceness of Siberian winters.

Remembered only far away in Moscow at the Tomb of the Unknown Soldier.

A monument to their memory or a shrine to the greed of man and the futility of war.

Waiting

The definition of "wait" according to Webster's dictionary is "to stay in place in expectation". So, if we think about it, we probably spend 80% of our lives waiting for something. My earliest memory of waiting is of my mother lifting me into the carrier on her bicycle to take me to junior school. When we got to school, we would sit in class waiting for the teacher. As you got to the end of junior school you were there waiting for senior school. There was lots of waiting in senior school. Waiting for your friends to walk home; waiting for lunchtime to go out to play, then waiting for exam results and culminating in the really tense waiting for leaving cert results. Then the wait to see if you get the choice you want to get in college. There are so many of the big events involve waiting. Waiting for the boyfriend's phone call, waiting for promotion, waiting for more exam results, waiting at the church, waiting for baby to arrive. Along with all the big waiting's, there are all the mundane ones, waiting for the bus, for the movie to start, for the meeting to begin. Life is really one big wait.

About the Author

Helen Mangan

Helen Mangan, the Bray-born author, proudly presents her literary concoction – with a dash of love, a sprinkle of wanderlust, and a spirit of adventure. The second-in-command of her original clan (Catherine, Eamon, and Michael), Helen has expertly juggled the family roles of wife to Frank, mum to her three fabulous offspring (Janice, Cliona, and Ciara), and two equally fabulous grand offspring (Molly and Hannah), who've had the privilege of globetrotting with her as if collecting passport stamps were a competitive sport.

In between her jet-setting adventures, Helen has been penning short stories and poems that capture the essence of her unpredictable life journey. Now, she's wrapping up all that wit and wisdom into this book – her gift to the world. Let's raise a glass (or a book) to Helen, whose tales are bound to have you chuckling, nodding in agreement, or frantically calling your siblings to confirm that you're definitely the favourite.

Printed in Great Britain
by Amazon

36454315R00071